BABY BEAR'S CHAIRS

written by
JANE YOLEN

illustrated by
MELISSA SWEET

GULLIVER BOOKS • HARCOURT, INC.
Orlando Austin New York San Diego Toronto London

Requests for permission to make copies of any part
of the work should be mailed to the following address:
Permissions Department, Harcourt, Inc.,
6277 Sea Harbor Drive, Orlando, Florida 32887-6777.

www.HarcourtBooks.com

Gulliver Books is a trademark of Harcourt, Inc., registered
in the United States of America and/or other jurisdictions.

Library of Congress Cataloging-in-Publication Data
Yolen, Jane.
Baby Bear's chairs/Jane Yolen; illustrated by Melissa Sweet.
p. cm.
"Gulliver Books."
Summary: Baby Bear's favorite "chair" is his father's chest or lap,
just before his father puts him to bed.
[1. Father and child—Fiction. 2. Chairs—Fiction. 3. Bedtime—Fiction.
4. Bears—Fiction. 5. Stories in rhyme.] I. Sweet, Melissa, ill. II. Title.
PZ8.3.Y76Bab 2005
[E]—dc22 2004012227
ISBN 0-15-205114-7

First edition

H G F E D C B A

Printed in Singapore

The illustrations in this book were done in mixed media
and collage on watercolor paper.
The display type was set in Kosmic.
The text type was set in Kosmic.
Color separations by Colourscan Co. Pte. Ltd., Singapore
Printed and bound by Tien Wah Press, Singapore
This book was printed on totally chlorine-free
Stora Enso Matte paper.
Production supervision by Ginger Boyer
Designed by Jessica Dacher and Scott Piehl

To my baby bears: Wee David, Caroline known
as CC, and Amelia sometimes called Moo—J. Y.

To Liz and Lily—M. S.

Some bears sit
in great big chairs,
great big chairs
for great big bears.

And great big bears
have so much fun,
they're never told
that playtime's done.

And being bears
both big and great,
at night they also
stay up late.

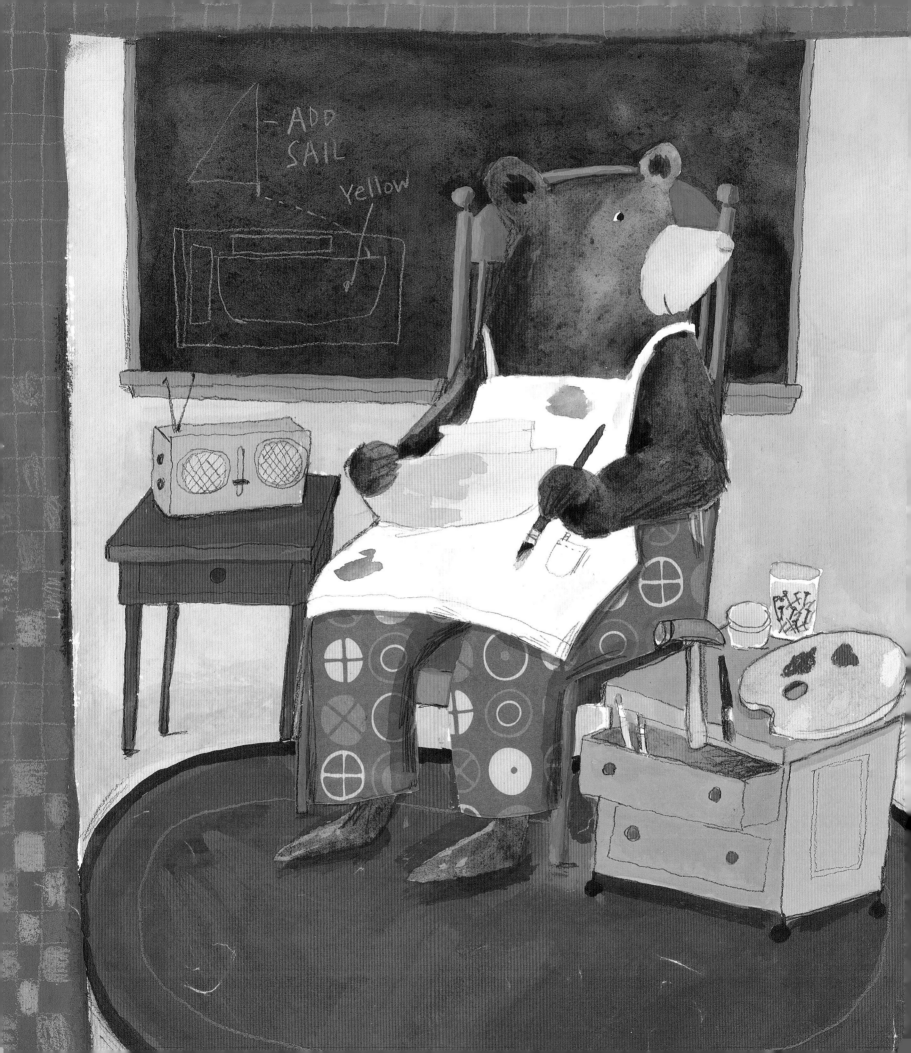

Not like other bears
I know,
who right at one
to nap must go.

Some bears sit
in middling chairs,
middling chairs
for middling bears,

pretending that
the chair's a ship
for bears who like
to take a trip.

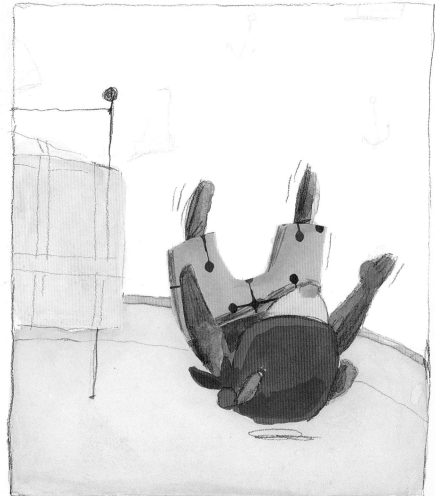

And middling bears
in middling chairs
are bears who like
to take on dares—

like running fast
and jumping high.
And when they fall,
they never cry.

Not like other bears
who trip
and fall off chairs
when *they* play ship.

Some bears sit
in tiny chairs,
tiny chairs
for tiny bears.

Though tiny chairs
can be quite tall,
with straps so
tiny bears don't fall.

And in high chairs,
with tiny paws
the bears draw pictures
with their claws,

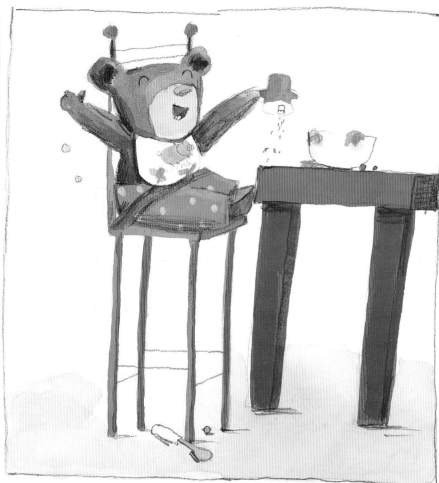

or drop their spoons,
and other stuff
until their mama's
had enough.

Yet still, of all the chairs,
the best
is when I lie
on Papa's chest,

or cuddle up
to take a nap
upon the chair
that's Papa's lap.

There no one warns me,
"Stop!" or "Go!"
Or loudly calls out,
"Baby—no!"

My papa's lap
is just for me
till I'm as big
a bear as he.

And when I am
asleep at last
upon the chair
that holds me fast,

then Papa brings me
up the stairs
to sleep all night
among big bears.

Night-night,
bear hug tight,
snuggle down
till morning's light.

Good night, bears.